D1546242

MYSTERY STORIES

ELIZABETH PETERS

MYSTERIOUSPRESS.COM

OPEN ROAD

INTEGRATED MEDIA

NEW YORK

"Liz Peters, PI" first published in *Christmas Stalkings*, edited by Charlotte MacLeod, 1991; "The Locked Tomb Mystery" first published in *Sisters in Crime*, edited by Marilyn Wallace, 1989; "The Runaway" (as Barbara Michaels) first published in *Sisters in Crime*, edited by Marilyn Wallace, 1989.

Cover design by Andy Ross

ISBN: 978-1-5040-5551-2

Published in 2018 by MysteriousPress.com/Open Road Integrated Media, Inc.
180 Maiden Lane
New York, NY 10038
www.openroadmedia.com

CONTENTS

LIZ PETERS, PI

I did not have a hangover. Those rumors about me aren't true; they are spread by people who are jealous of my ability to handle the hard stuff. The truth is, I can polish off three giant-sized Hershey bars before bedtime and wake clear-eyed as a baby.

All the same, I wasn't at my best that morning. When I put my pants on, one leg at a time (I always do it that way), my heel caught in the hem, and then the zipper jammed and I broke a fingernail trying to free it. The weather was lousy—gray and bleak and dripping cold rain that didn't have the guts to turn into snow. On Christmas Eve, yet. You'd think that the Big Gal Up There would have the decency to provide a white Christmas. I didn't count on it. I don't count on much.

My office was pretty depressing too. The velvety bloom on the flat surfaces wasn't the winter light. It was dust. My cleaning woman hadn't shown up that week.

1

I work out of my house because it's more convenient; I mean, hauling a word processor and printer around with you gets to be a drag. I'm a mystery writer. It's a dirty job, and nobody really has to do it. I do it because it's preferable to jobs like embalming and mucking out stables. They say a writer's life is a lonely one. That's a crock of doo-doo. I've got enough of a rep so that people come to me. Too darned many of them, but then that's the way it goes in my business. Too darned many people. You could say the same thing about the world in general, if you were philosophically inclined. Which I am.

You might ask why, if my profession is that of writer, I call myself a PI. (You might ask, but you might not get an answer. It's nobody's business what I call myself.) The truth is, I don't know how I got myself into this private-investigating sideline. It sure as heck wasn't for the money. Everybody knows PIs can't make a living; look at their clothes, their scrungy living quarters, their beat-up cars. Some of the gals can't even afford to buy a hat. So why did I do it? Simple. Because it was there—the dirt, the filth, the injustice, the pain. All of suffering humanity, bleeding and hurting and crying for help. When one of them bled on my rug, I had to do something. I mean, what the heck, that rug set me back a bundle. It's an antique Bokhara. I should let people bleed all over it?

I have to admit it wasn't a pretty sight that morning. Dust, dog hairs, cigarette ashes, and a few other disgusting objects (including the dogs themselves) dulled its deep-crimson sheen. After a cup of the brew, with all the trimmings—that's how I drink it, and if people want to make something of it, let them— my eyeballs felt a little less like hard-boiled eggs. I lit a cigarette. What the heck, you only die once. My desk squatted there like an archaeological mound, layers-deep in the accumulated gar- bage of living. I had to step over a couple of bodies to get to it. There was another limp carcass on my chair. When I moved it, it bit me. So what was one more scar? I'm covered with them. That's the way it goes in my business. Cats are only one of the hazards. The dogs are no picnic either. They don't bite, but I keep falling over them.

I sat down on the chair and lit a cigarette. The blank screen of the word processor stared at me like the eye of a dead Cyclops. My stomach twisted like a hanged man spinning on the end of a rope. Shucks, I thought. Here we go again. I forced my fingers onto the keyboard. It was like that every morning. It never got easier, it never would. There are no words. That was the trouble—no words. At least not in what passes for my brain. But somehow I had to come up with a few thousand of them, spell them right, put them into the guts of the machine and hope they came out making sense. That's my job. There are worse ones—performing autopsies and cleaning litter boxes, for example. But at 9 A.M. on a dreary winter morning on a mean street in Maryland, with dust and cat hairs clogging my sinuses and a couple of dogs scratching fleas, and my head as empty as Dan Quayle's, I couldn't think of one. I lit a cigarette.

The coffee cup was scummed with cold froth and the ash- tray was a reeking heap of butts when I came out of my stupor to see that there were words on the screen in front of me. They seemed to be spelled right, too. I wondered, vaguely, what had interrupted the creative flow—and then I heard the footsteps. Heavy, halting steps, coming nearer and nearer, down the dim hallways of the house, inexorably approaching. . . . I looked at the dogs. They're supposed to bark when somebody comes to the door. They never do. If I hadn't heard them snoring I'd have thought they were dead.

Closer and closer came the footsteps. Slower and slower. He was deliberately prolonging the suspense, making me wait. I took one hand off the keyboard and pushed the shining waves of thick bronze hair away from my brow.

The lamp on the desk beside me cast a bright pool of light across the keyboard, but the rest of the room was dark with winter shadows. He was a darker shadow, bulky and silent. I lit a cigarette.

"Hey, Jaz," I said. "Got time for some—"

He didn't. He was a big man. When he hit the floor he raised a cloud of dust that fogged the lamplight and my sinuses. Got to call that cleaning woman, I mused between sneezes. She was Jaz's cousin, or grandmother, or something. He'd found her for me. He was always doing things like that for me. He always had time for some . . .

I got to my feet and looked over the desk. He lay face down, unmoving. A film of gray covered his thick black hair. I know what death looks like. I've dealt with it . . . how many times? Forty, fifty times, maybe more. I can handle it. But I found myself thinking I was glad he'd fallen forward, so I couldn't see his face—the strong white teeth bared, not in his friendly grin but in a final grimace of pain, the soft brown eyes fixed and staring and filmed with dog hairs . . . Call me sentimental, if you want, but dusty eyeballs still get to me.

As I stood there, fighting those softer feelings that hide deep inside all us mystery writers who moon-light as private investigators, despite our efforts to build a tough shell so we can deal with the sick, disgusting, hideous realities of life without losing our integrity or our nerve and go on with our jobs of removing an occasional small piece of filthy slime from the world so it's a better place, if only infinitesimally so . . . Anyhow, after I had wiped my eyes on my sleeve, a little spark of light winked at me from the center of his broad back.

I had to push the dogs away before I could kneel beside him. They're so doggone stupid. They couldn't even tell he was dead. They were nudging him, wanting him to get up and play, as he always did.

It could have been a jeweled decoration or medal, if it had been on his chest instead of his back. The colorless stones glimmered palely in the dusky room. They weren't diamonds or even rhinestones. They were glass. I should know. I had only paid ten bucks for the hatpin. I collect hatpins. Just one of my little weaknesses. The last time I'd seen this particular specimen . . . I couldn't remember when it was. Had it been in the porcelain holder with the others, the last time I looked? Trouble was, I hadn't really looked. You don't look at familiar objects, things that have been in their places for weeks or months or years. You just assume they're there, the way they always have been. I recognized it, though—the head of it, I mean—and I knew only too well what the rest of it was like. Ten inches of polished metal, rigid and deadly. In Victorian days they passed laws limiting the length of the pins women used to hold those enormous hats in place. Ironic, I thought, lighting another cigarette. Men turn purple with outrage when some legislator tries to keep them from stockpiling Uzis, but a woman couldn't even own a lousy hatpin . . .

The mind plays funny tricks on you when a friend drops dead on your floor. I was wondering whether there were still laws on the books banning hatpins when I heard something that woke me up like a dash of icy water in the face. Mine is the last house on a dead-end road, out in the country, so when I hear a car I know it's heading for me. This one was coming too fast, tires screeching around the steep downhill curve. I got to the window in time to see it slow for the sharp turn into my driveway. Amazing. He'd had sense enough not to use the siren. He can never resist the flasher, though; it spun like a dying sun, sending red beams through the rain.

It was like a thick curtain had been yanked away, clearing my head; I saw it all, clear as a printed warrant. I'd been set up. But good. A dead man in my study, my hatpin through his heart, and the fuzz tipped off in time to catch me red-handed. (A figure of speech we PIs use; there wasn't much blood, and I hadn't been stupid enough to touch the body.) I was in deep doo-doo, though. That wasn't generalized fuzz, it was my nemesis, Sheriff Bludger. We had tangled before, on issues like gun control, and he wasn't awfully crazy about little me. A thick-headed rednecked male chauvinist, he would be drooling at the prospect of catching me with my hatpin in somebody's back.

The cruiser swung into the driveway and accelerated, sending the gravel flying. One of the cats growled. I looked at him. "Hold 'em off, Diesel," I snapped. He jumped off the windowsill and headed for the back door. The dogs were already there, stupid tails wagging. They could hardly wait to jump all over the nice cops and lick their hands and bring them balls to throw. The dogs were about as much use as fuzzy bunnies, but as I grabbed my purse I saw that Diesel had rallied the rest of the cats, six of them in all. They were all inside that day on account of the rain. Diesel himself weighs almost twenty pounds, and Bludger suffers from terminal ailurophobia. I figured I had maybe three minutes.

I went out the front door while Bludger and Company were trying to get in the back. Unfortunately the Caddy was also in the back. I circled carefully around the house, shivering as the cold rain stung my face, and crept through the shrubbery till I reached the garage. Peering around the corner, I saw the cruiser parked by the back steps. The back door was open, and from inside I could hear a lot of noise—dogs barking and men cursing. There was no sound from the cats. Unlike dogs and rattlesnakes, they don't warn you before they strike. They aren't gentlemen. That's one of the reasons why I like them.

The Caddy purrs like a kitten and turns on a dime. I was out of the garage and heading down the drive before Bludger got wind of what was happening. Darned fool—if he'd left the cruiser blocking the gate I'd have been in big trouble, but no, he had to come right up to the door. That big beer belly of his makes him reluctant to walk farther than he has to, I guess. It was wobbling like a bowl of custard when he came barreling out of the back door, waving his stupid little gun and yelling. I waved back as I sent the Caddy shooting through the gate.

I pushed a lock of shining bronze hair out of my eyes and shoved my foot down hard on the gas. The car roared up the hill like a rocket, taking the curves like the sweet lady she is. You can have your Porsches and Ferraris; I always say there's nothing like a Cadillac brougham for eluding the cops. Not that I was up for a high-speed chase across the county. Excessive speed is socially irresponsible, and besides, Bludger could cut me off at the pass; he knew the back roads as well as I did and he had plenty of manpower. I had to get out of sight, but fast—within the next thirty seconds—and I knew just how to do it.

I'm not given to praying, but I sent a passionate petition to the patron saint of private eyes as I thundered toward the stop sign at the top of the hill. She came through for me; the main road was clear. Instead of turning right or left, I hit the brake and sent the Caddy slithering *across* the road and up the bank on the opposite shoulder. A big green-and-white construction trailer stood there; the bridge across the creek had been finished three months earlier, but they hadn't got around to removing the trailer. Typical. And lucky for me. I barely made it, though. A couple of inches of my back fender were still visible when the cruiser appeared, but Bludger didn't notice. He was too busy trying to figure out which way I had turned. The decision was easy, even for his limited brain; a right turn would have taken me onto the bridge and a mile-long stretch of straight road. To the left the road rises and curves. He went left.

I waited till he was out of sight. Fastening my seat belt, which I hadn't had time to do before, I backed out of my hiding place and headed across the bridge. I have to admit my pulse was pretty fast; this was the tricky part, if Bludger got smart and turned back too soon, he'd see me. I couldn't stay where I was for the same reason, the Caddy would have been visible to a car coming down the hill.

Saint Kinsey was still with me. Across the bridge and over the hill, to Grandmother's house we go . . . The driveway was a rutted track, with only a few grains of gravel remaining, the house looked like an abandoned ruin. She came out on the sagging porch, her shotgun over her arm, squinting through the rain. When she recognized me, a toothless grin split the wrinkled face under the faded sunbonnet.

"Hey, Liz. Got time for—"

"No, Grannie." I slung my purse over my shoulder. "I need to borrow the pickup. If Bludger finds the Caddy, tell him I stole your truck, okay?"

Grannie spat neatly into the weeds beside the steps. "Keys are in the ignition. Leave yours; I'll pull the Caddy into the shed after you go."

Movement at the window caught my eye. Something fluttered against the pane, like a trapped moth. A hand—too small and thin, too pale . . . I swallowed hard and waved back. "How's Danny doing?"

"Okay. That wheelchair you got him was a big help. Don't s'pose you've got time to come in and say hello? He don't see many folks, and he's crazy about you . . ."

"That's 'cause he don't see many folks." I forced a smile, directed it at the window, where Danny's small pale face was pressed to the glass. The wheelchair might have been a help, but it was a heck of a Christmas present for a kid. I'd tied a big red bow across the seat and then ripped it off—too much of a contrast between holiday cheer and sad reality—one of those ironic contrasts we PIs keep seeing all around us . . .

I swallowed harder, stuck my cold hands in the pockets of my jeans. My fingers touched something soft. I pulled it out. It was a little squashed, but Danny and I had agreed we liked chocolate that way. "Give him this, Grannie. As a token of better things to come. Tell him—tell him I'll be back to spend Christmas Eve with him."

Grannie's rheumy eyes opened as wide as her wrinkled lids allowed—not much. "But, Liz, it's your spare. What'll you do without—"

"I'll manage," I said gruffly. "No big deal. See you later, Grannie—unless I'm in the slammer."

She offered me the shotgun, the sunbonnet, and the dirt-colored sweater she had thrown over her shoulders. I took the last two, winked at her, and headed for the truck.

Heading south on 75 I met two cruisers heading north. I smiled without humor. The county crooks would have a field day today, beating up their wives and dealing drugs and driving drunk unmolested; Bludger would have every available cop out looking for harmless little old me.

I'd had my eye on Bludger for months. I couldn't believe he was as stupid as he looked; but if he wasn't up to his thick neck in the drug traffic, why did he keep getting in my face very time I tried to nail a local dealer? Over the past years, drug traffic in the county had increased a hundredfold. It wasn't just kids and adult delinquents growing marijuana in woodland clearings, it was crack and coke brought in by big-city dealers who found lucrative markets and safer operations out in the boonies. Every now and then Bludger would round up some kids from the Projects, and there'd be a big hurrah in the local paper. But I knew, and Bludger should have known, that that wasn't going to solve the problem. The people who lived in the Projects weren't supporting a million-dollar industry. The buyers had to be people with money, and they weren't buying off the streets.

I had a personal interest in the drug biz. It lost me a darned good cleaning woman—Danny's mom. She was sixteen when she had Danny, after a hasty marriage to a scuzzball who beat her up with monotonous regularity before he got bored with the entertainment and walked out on her. Three kids (two of them died, don't ask how), no education, no skills—it's a wonder she stuck it out as long as she did. It was after the second baby died that she started doing drugs. Eventually, inevitably, they killed her. So now Grannie was trying to raise a seven-year-old on nothing a month and I was stuck with a lazy incompetent for a cleaning woman. You understand, it was the inconvenience that ticked me off. Not sentimentality. We tough female writer-PIs aren't sentimental.

Grannie's pickup made a noise like a tractor. I encouraged it onto the freeway ramp and headed east toward Baltimore. A couple of miles and I'd be over the county line. Not that that would do me much good; Bludger would certainly have alerted the state cops as well as his counterparts next door. I drove at about forty, not because I was trying to avoid traffic cops but because that was as fast as the pickup would go.

There had to be some connection between Jaz's murder and my recent investigations. Could it be Bludger himself who had set me up? I'd talked to Jaz about my suspicions, after he told me about a friend of his who'd been arrested for dealing dope down in D.C. (These days it's hard to find someone who doesn't know someone who's been arrested for dealing dope down in D.C.) Would Bludger commit murder just to get me off the trail? Not unless I was sniffing right at his heels. If I was, I sure as heck didn't know it.

The sleety rain was falling harder and the windshield wipers seemed to be suffering from mechanical arthritis. I decided I'd better get off the road. Pulling into a McDonald's, I ordered coffee and a Big Mac with everything (what the heck, you can only die once) and parked.

I always get my best ideas when I'm eating. Don't know why that is. Maybe cholesterol stimulates the brain cells. After finishing my Big Mac I lit a cigarette and drove on to the shopping center. It was all decorated for Christmas—had been since mid-October—and it was the most depressing darned sight I had ever seen. The plastic wreaths and garlands had faded to a sickly chartreuse; they hung like dead parrots from lampposts and storefronts. Rain dripped drearily off the shiny red plastic bows. Strategically spotted speakers blared out that lovely classic carol, "I Saw Mommy Kissing Santa Claus." Next on the agenda, no doubt, would be "All I Want for Christmas Is My Two Front Teeth," or "I Don't Care Who You Are, Fatty, Get Those Reindeer off My Roof." I swallowed the tide of sickness rising in my throat and reminded myself to replenish my supply of Di-Gel. We PIs buy a lot of antacids. Especially around Christmas.

I miss the old-fashioned telephone booths, with doors you can close, but Grannie's sunbonnet was a big help; it kept the rain off my face and kept passersby from hearing my end of the conversation.

First I called Jaz's office. Mary Jo was on that day. She wanted to talk, but I cut her short. I sure as heck didn't want to be the one to tell her about Jaz. I asked her where he was due to be that morning, before he came to me. Some of the names I knew, some I didn't. But they made a pattern. After I hung up I called

Rick. He wanted to talk too. Everybody wants to talk. I told him what I wanted. He gasped. "G—d d—n it, Liz—"

"Watch your mouth, Rick. You know my readers don't like dirty words."

"Oh—oh, yeah. Sorry. But what—"

"Never mind what. Just be there. I've cracked the case. You can make the arrest. I don't want the credit. I never do."

"But—"

I hung up.

Rick already owed me a couple. This would make three—no, four. You could call our relationship a social one—at least you'd better call it that. We'd met at a party, one of those boring Washington affairs writers get sucked into; I was sulking in a corner, nursing my drink and wondering how soon I could cut out, when I saw him. And he saw me. Our eyes met, across the room . . . Later, we got to talking. He asked me what I did for a living, I politely reciprocated—and that's how it began. He'd been promoted a couple of times since I started helping him out and he was man enough to give me credit—privately, if not to his boss at the Agency—so I knew he'd respond this time.

It would take him an hour or more to get there, though. I dawdled in the drugstore, picked up a package of Di-Gel and a few other odds and ends I figured I would need, and then headed back to town at a leisurely thirty miles per hour. The rain slid like tears down the cracked facade of the windshield. Tears for a good man gone bad, for a sick world that teaches kids to get high and cop out. I felt sick myself. I chewed a Di-Gel and lit a cigarette.

I had to circle the block three times before I found the parking spot I wanted, right across from the sheriff's office. No hurry. Rick wouldn't be there for another half hour, and I sure as heck wasn't walking into the lion's den without him. I'm tough, and I'm smart, but I'm not stupid. I ate a couple of Hershey bars while I thumbed through the latest issue of *Victorian Homes.* Then I lit a cigarette. I had smoked three of them before Rick showed up. I watched him as he trotted up the stairs. He was a big man. (I like big men.) I waited till he'd gone in, then pulled my sunbonnet over my head and followed.

A fresh kid in a trooper's uniform tried to stop me when I headed for Bludger's office. I straight-armed him out of the way and went on in. Rick was sitting on the edge of the desk and Bludger was yelling at him. He hates having people sit on the edge of his desk. When he saw me, his face turned purple. "D—n it, Grannie, how'd you get past—"

"I don't allow talk like that," I told him, whipping off my sunbonnet. "And I'm not Grannie."

His eyes bulged till they looked like they'd roll out of the sockets. Rick was grinning, but he looked a little anxious. The third man started to stand up, and fell back into his chair with a groan. I sat down on the other corner of Bludger's desk.

"Hi, Jaz," I said. "Feeling better?"

Bludger got his voice back. "You're under arrest," he bellowed.

I raised one eyebrow. "What's the charge?"

"Attempted murder!"

"With this?" I picked up the plasticine envelope. The hatpin had been cut down from ten inches to about two. "Darn it," I said. "I paid ten bucks for this. It's ruined."

"You shoved that thing into him—" Bludger began.

"Is that what he says?" I looked at Jaz.

He ran his fingers through his thick dark hair. "I don't . . . I can't remember . . ."

I lit a cigarette. "Oh, yeah? Well, let me refresh your memory. You stuck that pin into your own back just before you walked into my house. It's three and a half miles from the previous stop on your schedule; you couldn't possibly have driven that far without noticing that you had a sharp object in your back. My cleaning woman is a friend of yours; she stole that hatpin for you, several days ago. I was getting too close, wasn't I, Jaz? And I made the mistake of discussing my ideas with you—my questions about how drugs were being delivered in the county. What better delivery system than good old reliable National Express? You're on the road every day, covering the same territory. You've got your own private delivery schedule, haven't you?"

His eyes narrowed. I wondered why I'd never noticed before how empty they were, like pale marbles in the head of a wax dummy. "You're bluffing," he snarled. "You can't prove—"

"I never bluff," I told him, brushing a lock of shining auburn hair away from my forehead. "The truck will be clean, but you had to package the garbage somewhere. Your own apartment probably. I'd try the kitchen first, Bludger. There'll be traces left. Men don't know how to clean a kitchen properly. And, as I have reason to know, neither does Jaz's 'cousin.'"

I didn't expect him to break so fast. He got to his feet and started toward me. Rick moved to intercept him, but I shook my head. "Don't dirty your hands, Rick. Come any closer, Jaz, and you get this cigarette right in the face."

"You don't understand," he groaned. "It was her idea. She made me do it."

"Sure," I said bitterly. "Blame the dame. You and that MCP Adam."

"Adam?" He looked like a dead fish, eyes bulging, mouth ajar. "How many guys do you have dropping by for some—"

"Never mind." It was all clear to me now. I felt a little sick. Men, I thought bitterly. You try to be nice, offer a guy some milk and cookies, listen to his troubles, and he starts getting ideas.

I lit a cigarette. "He's all yours, boys. You'll have to figure out who has jurisdiction."

"I'm sheriff of this county," Bludger blustered.

"I wouldn't be surprised if a state line got crossed," Rick drawled. "And the DEA has jurisdiction—"

"Fight it out between yourselves," I told them. "Frankly, I don't give a darn."

Jaz dropped back onto his chair, face hidden in his hands. A lock of thick black hair curled over his fingers. I headed, fast, for the door.

Rick followed me out. "What say I drop by later for some—"

"You're all alike," I said bitterly. "Wave a chocolate-chip cookie in front of you and you'll do anything, say anything."

He captured my hand. "For one of your chocolate-chip cookies I would. They're special, Liz. Like you."

"Sorry, Rick." I freed my hand so I could light another cigarette. "I've got a chapter to finish. That's what it's all about, you know. The real world. Putting words on paper, spelling them right . . . All the rest of it is just fun and games. Just . . ."

The words stuck in my throat. Rick leaned over to look into my face. "You're not crying, are you?"

"Who, me? PIs don't cry." I tossed the cigarette away. It spun in a glowing arc through the curtain of softly falling snow. Snow. Big fat flakes like fragments of foam rubber. They clung to my long lashes. I blinked. "Rick. Isn't there a reward for breaking this case?"

Rick blinked. He has long thick lashes too. (I like long thick lashes in a man.) "Yeah. Some guy whose kid died of an overdose offered it. It's yours, I guess. Enough to buy a lot of cigarettes and chocolate chips."

I took his arm. "You'll get your chocolate chip cookies, Rick. But first we're going shopping. Toys 'R' Us, and then a breeder I know whose golden retriever has just had a litter. A tree, a great big one, with all the trimmings, the fattest turkey Safeway has left . . . Pick up your feet, Rick. We've got a lot to do. It's Christmas Eve—and it's snowing!"

I lit a cigarette. What the heck, you only live once.

THE LOCKED
TOMB MYSTERY

S enebtisi's funeral was the talk of southern Thebes. Of
course, it could not compare with the burials of Great Ones
and Pharaohs, whose Houses of Eternity were furnished with
gold and fine linen and precious gems, but ours was not a quar-
ter where nobles lived; our people were craftsmen and small
merchants, able to afford a chamber-tomb and a coffin and a
few spells to ward off the perils of the Western Road—no more
than that. We had never seen anything like the burial of the old
woman who had been our neighbor for so many years.

The night after the funeral, the customers of Nehi's tavern
could talk of nothing else. I remember that evening well. For one
thing, I had just won my first appointment as a temple scribe. I
was looking forward to boasting a little, and perhaps paying for
a round of beer, if my friends displayed proper appreciation of
my good fortune. Three of the others were already at the tavern

when I arrived, my linen shawl wrapped tight around me. The weather was cold even for winter, with a cruel, dry wind driving sand into every crevice of the body.

"Close the door quickly," said Senu, the carpenter. "What weather! I wonder if the Western journey will be like this—cold enough to freeze a man's bones."

This prompted a ribald comment from Rennefer, the weaver, concerning the effects of freezing on certain of Senebtisi's vital organs. "Not that anyone would notice the difference," he added. "There was never any warmth in the old hag. What sort of mother would take all her possessions to the next world and leave her only son penniless?"

"Is it true, then?" I asked, signaling Nehi to fetch the beer jar. "I have heard stories—"

"All true," said the potter, Baenre. "It is a pity you could not attend the burial, Wadjsen; it was magnificent!"

"You went?" I inquired. "That was good of you, since she ordered none of her funerary equipment from you."

Baenre is a scanty little man with thin hair and sharp bones. It is said that he is a domestic tyrant, and that his wife cowers when he comes roaring home from the tavern, but when he is with us, his voice is almost a whisper. "My rough kitchenware would not be good enough to hold the wine and fine oil she took to the tomb. Wadjsen, you should have seen the boxes and jars and baskets—dozens of them. They say she had a gold mask, like the ones worn by great nobles, and that all her ornaments were of solid gold."

"It is true," said Rennefer. "I know a man who knows one of the servants of Bakenmut, the goldsmith who made the ornaments."

"How is her son taking it?" I asked. I knew Minmose slightly; a shy, serious man, he followed his father's trade of stone carving. His mother had lived with him all his life, greedily scooping up his profits, though she had money of her own, inherited from her parents.

"Why, as you would expect," said Senu, shrugging. "Have you ever heard him speak harshly to anyone, much less his mother? She was an old she-goat who treated him like a boy who has not cut off the side lock; but with him it was always 'Yes, honored mother,' and 'As you say, honored mother.' She would not even allow him to take a wife."

"How will he live?"

"Oh, he has the shop and the business, such as it is. He is a hard worker; he will survive."

In the following months I heard occasional news of Minmose. Gossip said he must be doing well, for he had taken to spending his leisure time at a local house of prostitution— a pleasure he never had dared *enjoy* while his mother lived. Nefertiry, the loveliest and most expensive of the girls, was the object of his desire, and Rennefer remarked that the maiden must have a kind heart, for she could command higher prices than Minmose was able to pay. However, as time passed, I forgot Minmose and Senebtisi, and her rich burial. It was not until almost a year later that the matter was recalled to my attention.

The rumors began in the marketplace, at the end of the time of inundation, when the floodwater lay on the fields and the farmers were idle. They enjoy this time, but the police of the city do not; for idleness leads to crime, and one of the most popular crimes is tomb robbing. This goes on all the time in a small way, but when the Pharaoh is strong and stern, and the laws are strictly enforced, it is a very risky trade. A man stands to lose more than a hand or an ear if he is caught. He also risks damnation after he has entered his own tomb; but some men simply do not have proper respect for the gods.

The king, Nebmaatre (may he live forever!), was then in his prime, so there had been no tomb robbing for some time—or at least none had been detected. But, the rumors said, three men of west Thebes had been caught trying to sell ornaments such as are buried with the dead. The rumors turned out to be correct, for once. The men were questioned on the soles of their feet and confessed to the robbing of several tombs.

Naturally all those who had kin buried on the west bank—which included most of us—were alarmed by this news, and half the nervous matrons in our neighborhood went rushing across the river to make sure the family tombs were safe. I was not surprised to hear that that dutiful son Minmose had also felt obliged to make sure his mother had not been disturbed.

However, I was surprised at the news that greeted me when I paid my next visit to Nehi's tavern. The moment I entered, the others began to talk at once, each eager to be the first to tell the shocking *facts*.

"Robbed?" I repeated when I had sorted out the babble of voices. "Do you speak truly?"

"I do not know why you should doubt it," said Rennefer. "The richness of her burial was the talk of the city, was it not? Just what the tomb robbers like! They made a clean sweep of all the gold, and ripped the poor old hag's mummy to shreds."

At that point we were joined by another of the habitués, Merusir. He is a pompous, fat man who considers himself superior to the rest of us because he is Fifth Prophet of Amon. We put up with his patronizing ways because sometimes he knows court gossip. On that particular evening it was apparent that he was bursting with excitement. He listened with a supercilious sneer while we told him the sensational news. "I know, I know," he drawled. "I heard it much earlier—and with it, the other news which is known only to those in the confidence of the Palace."

He paused, ostensibly to empty his cup. Of course, we reacted as he had hoped we would, begging him to share the secret. Finally he condescended to inform us.

"Why, the amazing thing is not the robbery itself, but how it was done. The tomb entrance was untouched, the seals of the necropolis were unbroken. The tomb itself is entirely rock-cut, and there was not the slightest break in the walls or floor or ceiling. Yet when Minmose entered the burial chamber, he found the coffin open, the mummy mutilated, and the gold ornaments gone."

We stared at him, openmouthed.

"It is a most remarkable story," I said.

"Call me a liar if you like," said Merusir, who knows the language of polite insult as well as I do. "There was a witness—two, if you count Minmose himself. The sem-priest Wennefer was with him."

This silenced the critics. Wennefer was known to us all. There was not a man in southern Thebes with a higher reputation. Even Senebtisi had been fond of him, and she was not fond of many people. He had officiated at her funeral.

Pleased at the effect of his announcement, Merusir went on in his most pompous manner. "The king himself has taken an interest in the matter. He has called on Amenhotep Sa Hapu to investigate."

"Amenhotep?" I exclaimed. "But I know him well."

"You do?" Merusir's plump cheeks sagged like bladders punctured by a sharp knife.

Now, at that time Amenhotep's name was not in the mouth of everyone, though he had taken the first steps on that astonishing career that was to make him the intimate friend of Pharaoh. When I first met him, he had been a poor, insignificant priest at a local shrine. I had been sent to fetch him to the house where my master lay dead of a stab wound, presumably murdered. Amenhotep's fame had begun with that matter, for he had discovered the truth and saved an innocent man from execution. Since then he had handled several other cases, with equal success.

My exclamation had taken the wind out of Merusir's sails. He had hoped to impress us by telling us something we did not know. Instead it was I who enlightened the others about Amenhotep's triumphs. But when I finished, Rennefer shook his head.

"If this wise man is all you say, Wadjsen, it will be like inviting a lion to rid the house of mice. He will find there is a simple explanation. No doubt the thieves entered the burial chamber from above or from one side, tunneling through the rock. Minmose and Wennefer were too shocked to observe the hole in the wall, that is all."

We argued the matter for some time, growing more and more heated as the level of the beer in the jar dropped. It was a foolish argument, for none of us knew the facts; and to argue without knowledge is like trying to weave without thread.

This truth did not occur to me until the cool night breeze had cleared my head, when I was halfway home. I decided to pay Amenhotep a visit. The next time I went to the tavern, I would be the one to tell the latest news, and Merusir would be nothing!

Most of the honest householders had retired, but there were lamps burning in the street of the prostitutes, and in a few taverns. There was a light, as well, in one window of the house where Amenhotep lodged. Like the owl he resembled, with his beaky nose and large, close-set eyes, he preferred to work at night.

The window was on the ground floor, so I knocked on the wooden shutter, which of course was closed to keep out night demons. After a few moments the shutter opened, and the familiar nose appeared. I spoke my name, and Amenhotep went to open the door.

"Wadjsen! It has been a long time," he exclaimed. "Should I ask what brings you here, or shall I display my talents as a seer and tell you?"

"I suppose it requires no great talent," I replied. "The matter of Senebtisi's tomb is already the talk of the district."

"So I had assumed." He gestured me to sit down and hospitably indicated the wine jar that stood in the corner. I shook my head.

"I have already taken too much beer, at the tavern. I am sorry to disturb you so late—"

"I am always happy to see you, Wadjsen." His big dark eyes reflected the light of the lamp, so that they seemed to hold stars in their depths. "I have missed my assistant, who helped me to the truth in my first inquiry."

"I was of little help to you then," I said with a smile. "And in this case I am even more ignorant. The thing is a great mystery, known only to the gods."

"No, no!" He clapped his hands together, as was his habit when annoyed with the stupidity of his hearer. "There is no mystery. I know who robbed the tomb of Senebtisi. The only difficulty is to prove how it was done."

At Amenhotep's suggestion I spent the night at his house so that I could accompany him when he set out next morning to find the proof he needed. I required little urging, for I was afire with curiosity. Though I pressed him, he would say no more, merely remarking piously, "'A man may fall to ruin because of his tongue; if a passing remark is hasty and it is repeated, thou wilt make enemies.'"

I could hardly dispute the wisdom of this adage, but the gleam in Amenhotep's bulging black eyes made me suspect he took a malicious pleasure in my bewilderment.

After our morning bread and beer we went to the temple of Khonsu, where the sem-priest Wennefer worked in the records office. He was copying accounts from pottery ostraca onto a papyrus that was stretched across his lap. All scribes develop bowed shoulders from bending over their writing; Wennefer was folded almost double, his face scant inches from the surface of the papyrus. When Amenhotep cleared his throat, the old man started, smearing the ink. He waved our apologies aside and cleaned the papyrus with a wad of lint.

"No harm was meant, no harm is done," he said in his breathy, chirping voice. "I have heard of you, Amenhotep Sa Hapu; it is an honor to meet you."

"I, too, have looked forward to meeting you, Wennefer. Alas that the occasion should be such a sad one."

Wennefer's smile faded. "Ah, the matter of Senebtisi's tomb. What a tragedy! At least the poor woman can now have a proper reburial. If Minmose had not insisted on opening the tomb, her *ba* would have gone hungry and thirsty through eternity."

"Then the tomb entrance really was sealed and undisturbed?" I asked skeptically.

27

"I examined it myself," Wennefer said. "Minmose had asked me to meet him after the day's work, and we arrived at the tomb as the sun was setting; but the light was still good. I conducted the funeral service for Senebtisi, you know. I had seen the doorway blocked and mortared and with my own hands had helped to press the seals of the necropolis onto the wet plaster. All was as I had left it that day a year ago."

"Yet Minmose insisted on opening the tomb?" Amenhotep asked.

"Why, we agreed it should be done," the old man said mildly. "As you know, robbers sometimes tunnel in from above or from one side, leaving the entrance undisturbed. Minmose had brought tools. He did most of the work himself, for these old hands of mine are better with a pen than a chisel. When the doorway was clear, Minmose lit a lamp and we entered. We were crossing the hall beyond the entrance corridor when Minmose let out a shriek. 'My mother, my mother,' he cried—oh, it was pitiful to hear! Then I saw it too. The thing—the thing on the floor. . . ."

"You speak of the mummy, I presume," said Amenhotep. "The thieves had dragged it from the coffin out into the hall?"

"Where they despoiled it," Wennefer whispered. "The august body was ripped open from throat to groin, through the shroud and the wrappings and the flesh."

"Curious," Amenhotep muttered, as if to himself. "Tell me, Wennefer, what is the plan of the tomb?"

Wennefer rubbed his brush on the ink cake and began to draw on the back surface of one of the ostraca.

"It is a fine tomb, Amenhotep, entirely rock-cut. Beyond the entrance is a flight of stairs and a short corridor, thus leading to a hall broader than it is long, with two pillars. Beyond that, another short corridor; then the burial chamber. The august mummy lay here." And he inked in a neat circle at the beginning of the second corridor.

"Ha," said Amenhotep, studying the plan. "Yes, yes, I see. Go on, Wennefer. What did you do next?"

"I did nothing," the old man said simply. "Minmose's hand shook so violently that he dropped the lamp. Darkness closed in. I felt the presence of the demons who had defiled the dead. My tongue clove to the roof of my mouth and—"

"Dreadful," Amenhotep said. "But you were not far from the tomb entrance; you could find your way out?"

"Yes, yes, it was only a dozen paces; and by Amon, my friend, the sunset light has never appeared so sweet! I went at once to fetch the necropolis guards. When we returned to the tomb, Minmose had rekindled his lamp—"

"I thought you said the lamp was broken."

"Dropped, but fortunately not broken. Minmose had opened one of the jars of oil—Senebtisi had many such in the tomb, all of the finest quality—and had refilled the lamp. He had replaced the mummy in its coffin and was kneeling by it praying. Never was there so pious a son!"

"So then, I suppose, the guards searched for the tomb."

"We all searched," Wennefer said. "The tomb chamber was in a dreadful state; boxes and baskets had been broken open and the contents strewn about. Every object of precious metal had been stolen, including the amulets on the body."

"What about the oil, the linen, and the other valuables?" Amenhotep asked.

"The oil and the wine were in large jars, impossible to move easily. About the other things I cannot say; everything was in such confusion—and I do not know what was there to begin with. Even Minmose was not certain; his mother had filled and sealed most of the boxes herself. But I know what was taken from the mummy, for I saw the golden amulets and ornaments placed on it when it was wrapped by the embalmers. I do not like to speak evil of anyone, but you know, Amenhotep, that the embalmers . . ."

"Yes," Amenhotep agreed with a sour face. "I myself watched the wrapping of my father; there is no other way to make certain the ornaments will go on the mummy instead of into the coffers of the embalmers. Minmose did not perform this service for his mother?"

"Of course he did. He asked me to share in the watch, and I was glad to agree. He is the most pious—"

"So I have heard," said Amenhotep. "Tell me again, Wennefer, of the condition of the mummy. You examined it?"

"It was my duty. Oh, Amenhotep, it was a sad sight! The shroud was still tied firmly around the body; the thieves had cut straight through it and through the bandages beneath, baring the body. The arm bones were broken, so roughly had the thieves dragged the heavy gold bracelets from them."

"And the mask?" I asked. "It was said that she had a mask of solid gold."

"It, too, was missing."

"Horrible," Amenhotep said. "Wennefer, we have kept you from your work long enough. Only one more question. How do you think the thieves entered the tomb?"

The old man's eyes fell. "Through me," he whispered.

I gave Amenhotep a startled look. He shook his head warningly.

"It was not your fault," he said, touching Wennefer's bowed shoulder.

"It was. I did my best, but I must have omitted some vital part of the ritual. How else could demons enter the tomb?"

"Oh, I see." Amenhotep stroked his chin. "Demons."

"It could have been nothing else. The seals on the door were intact, the mortar untouched. There was no break of the smallest size in the stone of the walls or ceiling or floor."

"But—" I began.

"And there is this. When the doorway was clear and the light entered, the dust lay undisturbed on the floor. The only marks on it were the strokes of the broom with which Minmose, according to custom, had swept the floor as he left the tomb after the funeral service."

"Amon preserve us," I exclaimed, feeling a chill run through me.

Amenhotep's eyes moved from Wennefer to me, then back to Wennefer. "That is conclusive," he murmured.

"Yes," Wennefer said with a groan. "And I am to blame—I, a priest who failed at his task."

"No," said Amenhotep. "You did not fail. Be of good cheer, my friend. There is another explanation."

Wennefer shook his head despondently. "Minmose said the same, but he was only being kind. Poor man! He was so overcome, he could scarcely walk. The guards had to take him by the arms to lead him from the tomb. I carried his tools. It was the least—"

"The tools," Amenhotep interrupted. "They were in a bag or a sack?"

"Why, no. He had only a chisel and a mallet. I carried them in my hand as he had done."

Amenhotep thanked him again, and we took our leave. As we crossed the courtyard I waited for him to speak, but he remained silent; and after a while I could contain myself no longer.

"Do you still believe you know who robbed the tomb?"

"Yes, yes, it is obvious."

"And it was not demons?"

Amenhotep blinked at me like an owl blinded by sunlight.

"Demons are a last resort."

He had the smug look of a man who thinks he has said something clever; but his remark smacked of heresy to me, and I looked at him doubtfully.

"Come, come," he snapped. "Senebtisi was a selfish, greedy old woman, and if there is justice in the next world, as our faith decrees, her path through the Underworld will not be easy.

But why would diabolical powers play tricks with her mummy when they could torment her spirit? Demons have no need of gold."

"Well, but—"

"Your wits used not to be so dull. What do you think happened?"

"If it was not demons—"

"It was not."

"Then someone must have broken in."

"Very clever," said Amenhotep, grinning.

"I mean that there must be an opening, in the walls or the floor, that Wennefer failed to see."

"Wennefer, perhaps. The necropolis guards, no. The chambers of the tomb were cut out of solid rock. It would be impossible to disguise a break in such a surface, even if tomb robbers took the trouble to fill it in—which they never have been known to do."

"Then the thieves entered through the doorway and closed it again. A dishonest craftsman could make a copy of the necropolis seal. . . ."

"Good." Amenhotep clapped me on the shoulder. "Now you are beginning to think. It is an ingenious idea, but it is wrong. Tomb robbers work in haste, for fear of the necropolis guards. They would not linger to replace stones and mortar and seals."

"Then I do not know how it was done."

"Ah, Wadjsen, you are dense! There is only one person who could have robbed the tomb."

"I thought of that," I said stiffly, hurt by his raillery. "Minmose was the last to leave the tomb and the first to reenter it. He had good reason to desire the gold his mother should have left to him. But, Amenhotep, he could not have robbed the mummy on either occasion; there was not time. You know the funeral ritual as well as I. When the priests and mourners leave the tomb, they leave together. If Minmose had lingered in the burial chamber, even for a few minutes, his delay would have been noted and remarked upon."

"That is quite true," said Amenhotep.

"Also," I went on, "the gold was heavy as well as bulky. Minmose could not have carried it away without someone noticing."

"Again you speak truly."

"Then unless Wennefer the priest is conspiring with Minmose—"

"That good, simple man? I am surprised at you, Wadjsen. Wennefer is as honest as the Lady of Truth herself."

"Demons—"

Amenhotep interrupted with the hoarse hooting sound that passed for a laugh with him. "Stop babbling of demons. There is one man besides myself who knows how Senebtisi's tomb was violated. Let us go and see him."

He quickened his pace, his sandals slapping in the dust. I followed, trying to think. His taunts were like weights that pulled my mind to its farthest limits. I began to get an inkling of truth, but I could not make sense of it. I said nothing, not even when we turned into the lane south of the temple that led to the house of Minmose.

There was no servant at the door. Minmose himself answered our summons. I greeted him and introduced Amenhotep.

Minmose lifted his hands in surprise. "You honor my house, Amenhotep. Enter and be seated."

Amenhotep shook his head. "I will not stay, Minmose. I came only to tell you who desecrated your mother's tomb."

"What?" Minmose gaped at him. "Already you know? But how? It is a great mystery, beyond—"

"You did it, Minmose."

Minmose turned a shade paler. But that was not out of the way; even the innocent might blanch at such an accusation.

"You are mad," he said. "Forgive me, you are my guest, but—"

"There is no other possible explanation," Amenhotep said. "You stole the gold when you entered the tomb two days ago."

"But, Amenhotep," I exclaimed. "Wennefer was with him, and Wennefer saw the mummy already robbed when—"

"Wennefer did not see the mummy," Amenhotep said. "The tomb was dark; the only light was that of a small lamp, which Minmose promptly dropped. Wennefer has poor sight. Did you not observe how he bent over his writing? He caught only a glimpse of a white shape, the size of a wrapped mummy, before the light went out. When next Wennefer saw the mummy, it was in the coffin, and his view of it then colored his confused memory of the first supposed sighting of it. Few people are good observers. They see what they expect to see."

"Then what did he see?" I demanded. Minmose might not have been there. Amenhotep avoided looking at him.

"A piece of linen in the rough shape of a human form, arranged on the floor by the last person who left the tomb. It would have taken him only a moment to do this before he snatched up the broom and swept himself out."

"So the tomb was sealed and closed," I exclaimed. "For almost a year he waited—"

"Until the next outbreak of tomb robbing. Minmose could assume this would happen sooner or later; it always does. He thought he was being clever by asking Wennefer to accompany him—a witness of irreproachable character who could testify that the tomb entrance was untouched. In fact, he was too careful to avoid being compromised; that would have made me doubt him, even if the logic of the facts had not pointed directly at him. Asking that same virtuous man to share his supervision of the mummy wrapping, lest he be suspected of connivance with the embalmers; feigning weakness so that the necropolis guards would have to support him, and thus be in a position to swear he could not have concealed the gold on his person. Only a guilty man would be so anxious to appear innocent. Yet there was reason for his precautions. Sometime in the near future, when that loving son Minmose discovers a store of gold hidden in the house, overlooked by his mother—the old do forget sometimes—then, since men have evil minds, it might be necessary for Minmose to prove beyond a shadow of a doubt that he could not have laid hands on his mother's burial equipment."

Minmose remained dumb, his eyes fixed on the ground. It was I who responded as he should have, questioning and objecting.

"But how did he remove the gold? The guards and Wennefer searched the tomb, so it was not hidden there, and there was not time for him to bury it outside."

"No, but there was ample time for him to do what had to be done in the burial chamber after Wennefer had tottered off to fetch the guards. He overturned boxes and baskets, opened the coffin, ripped through the mummy wrappings with his chisel, and took the gold. It would not take long, especially for one who knew exactly where each ornament had been placed."

Minmose's haggard face was as good as an admission of guilt. He did not look up or speak, even when Amenhotep put a hand on his shoulder.

"I pity you, Minmose," Amenhotep said gravely. "After years of devotion and self-denial, to see yourself deprived of your inheritance . . . And there was Nefertiry. You had been visiting her in secret, even before your mother died, had you not? Oh, Minmose, you should have remembered the words of the sage: 'Do not go in to a woman who is a stranger; it is a great crime, worthy of death.' She has brought you to your death, Minmose. You knew she would turn from you if your mother left you nothing."

Minmose's face was gray. "Will you denounce me, then? They will beat me to make me confess."

"Any man will confess when he is beaten," said Amenhotep, with a curl of his lip. "No, Minmose, I will not denounce you. The court of the vizier demands facts, not theories, and you have covered your tracks very neatly. But you will not escape justice. Nefertiry will consume your gold as the desert sands drink water, and then she will cast you off; and all the while Anubis, the Guide of the Dead, and Osiris, the Divine Judge, will be waiting for you. They will eat your heart, Minmose, and your spirit will hunger and thirst through all eternity. I think your punishment has already begun. Do you dream, Minmose? Did you see your mother's face last night, wrinkled and withered, her sunken eyes accusing you, as it looked when you tore the gold mask from it?"

A long shudder ran through Minmose's body. Even his hair seemed to shiver and rise. Amenhotep gestured to me. We went away, leaving Minmose staring after us with a face like death.

After we had gone a short distance, I said, "There is one more thing to tell, Amenhotep."

"There is much to tell." Amenhotep sighed deeply. "Of a good man turned evil; of two women who, in their different ways, drove him to crime; of the narrow line that separates the virtuous man from the sinner. . . ."

"I do not speak of that. I do not wish to think of that. It makes me feel strange. . . . The gold, Amenhotep—how did Minmose bear away the gold from his mother's burial?"

"He put it in the oil jar," said Amenhotep. "The one he opened to get fresh fuel for his lamp. Who would wonder if, in his agitation, he spilled a quantity of oil on the floor? He has certainly removed it by now. He has had ample opportunity, running back and forth with objects to be repaired or replaced."

"And the piece of linen he had put down to look like the mummy?"

"As you well know," Amenhotep replied, "the amount of linen used to wrap a mummy is prodigious. He could have crumpled that piece and thrown it in among the torn wrappings. But I think he did something else. It was a cool evening, in winter, and Minmose would have worn a linen mantle. He took the cloth out in the same way he had brought it in. Who would notice an extra fold of linen over a man's shoulders?

"I knew immediately that Minmose must be the guilty party, because he was the only one who had the opportunity, but I did not see how he had managed it until Wennefer showed me where the supposed mummy lay. There was no reason for a thief to drag it so far from the coffin and the burial chamber—but Minmose could not afford to have Wennefer catch even a glimpse of that room, which was then undisturbed. I realized then that what the old man had seen was not the mummy at all, but a substitute."

"Then Minmose will go unpunished."

"I said he would be punished. I spoke truly." Again Amenhotep sighed.

"You will not denounce him to Pharaoh?"

"I will tell my lord the truth. But he will not choose to act. There will be no need."

He said no more. But six weeks later Minmose's body was found floating in the river. He had taken to drinking heavily, and people said he drowned by accident. But I knew it was otherwise. Anubis and Osiris had eaten his heart, just as Amenhotep had said.

Author's note: Amenhotep Sa Hapu was a real person who lived during the fourteenth century B.C. Later generations worshiped him as a sage and scholar; he seems like a logical candidate for the role of ancient Egyptian detective.

THE RUNAWAY

The younger girl was fifteen. She told people she was sixteen when they asked, but usually they didn't even bother. They just looked at her narrow shoulders and flat chest and skinny legs, and shook their heads. Mary knew they probably thought she was about twelve or thirteen. Nobody would hire a kid that age, and she couldn't show any proof she was older. The problem was that she wasn't old enough.

Some of the men would have hired Angie. She was almost seventeen and she was pretty. "Angie is the pretty one," their mother always said. Angie's best feature was her hair, long and smooth and shiny as yellow silk. *Flat* and *skinny* were words nobody would apply to Angie. The cloth of her tight jeans was straining at every seam. That was where the men looked—at the seat of Angie's jeans and the lush curves that pushed out the front of her shirt. Angie couldn't understand why Mary wouldn't let her take jobs from the men who looked at her that way.

Though she was the younger of the two, Mary had always been the one who looked after Angie, instead of the other way around. Angie was . . . sensitive. Angie didn't understand some things. And when she was scared or unhappy, she stuck out her lip and made whimpering noises, like a homesick puppy.

She was whimpering now. Mary didn't blame her. She was scared, too, but she couldn't let Angie see that she was. One of them had to be tough.

It was so dark! Nights in town were never like this. There were always streetlights, lighted windows, cars passing by. They hadn't seen a car for a long time, not since they'd turned off the highway onto the narrow country road. The last house had been at least a mile back.

To make matters worse, there was a storm coming on. Heavy clouds obscured moon and stars. So far the rain had held off, but lightning and thunder were getting closer, louder. The wind made queer rustling noises in the bushes along the road. There were other noises that couldn't have been made by the wind, but Mary didn't mention them. Angie was upset enough already. She couldn't go much farther; she was scared to death of lightning. They had to find shelter soon.

As Mary looked anxiously around her, she tripped and fell. Gravel stung her palms, and something sharp, a stone or a piece of broken glass, ripped into her knee. She bit her lip and managed not to cry out.

Angie was the one who yelled. "Mary, what's the matter? Get up, get up, I can't—"

"I tripped, that's all." Mary staggered to her feet and reached for Angie's hand. "Shut up, Angie. Someone will hear you."

"I don't care if they do. I don't like this. We should have gone to that house back there."

"And have them call the cops?" Mary forced herself to limp forward. Angie hung back, dragging at Mary's arm, and Mary lost her temper. "Damn it, Angie, this whole thing was your idea. You want to give up?"

"No, I won't go back. You know what he'll do. You promised! You said you'd take care of everything—"

"I've done all right so far, haven't I?" Mary demanded, stung by the note of criticism in her sister's voice.

"It was fun at first. But I told you we shouldn't've gone down this road."

"We wouldn't have had to if you hadn't come on to that sleazy character in the pizza place," Mary said. "He was following us—you, I mean."

"He was kind of cute," Angie said.

Mary was about to reply when a bolt of lightning split the sky and thunder rolled over them. Angie screamed.

"It's okay," Mary said, trying to steady her voice. "But we'd better walk faster. I don't want to be caught in the rain any more than you do. This damned road has to end up someplace."

Angie was genuinely terrified by lightning. She stumbled on, sobbing noisily, clutching Mary's hand till it ached.

Her distress softened Mary, as it always did. She got mad at Angie sometimes, but it was impossible to stay mad at her, she was so damned helpless. Giggling and grinning at that guy in the pizza place . . . Angie didn't know any better. She trusted everybody, even men whose eyes held that cold hunger when they looked at her. But she had a stubborn streak. When she had threatened to run away from home, Mary knew she meant it, and the thought of Angie out on her own, with no one to look after her, was too awful. She had had no choice but to go along. She wasn't all that crazy about what was happening at home, either.

Two hundred dollars—the savings of several years of baby-sitting—had seemed like a lot of money. But the bus fares had taken a big chunk; Mary wouldn't hitchhike, although Angie wanted to. And food cost a lot more than she had expected. Angie ate such a lot. As soon as they got jobs, everything would be all right, but so far they hadn't had any luck. Either people turned them down cold or the men looked at Angie in that hungry way.

And now, thanks to Angie's dumb stunt, they were lost on a dark country road with a storm about to cut loose. Mary wondered what time it was. It had been almost ten when they left the pizza place. It must be the middle of the night now. Her knee burned, and Angie kept dragging at her hand. She felt as if she weighed a ton.

Another flash of lightning won a squeal from Angie. Mary stopped. "There's a house over there. I saw it in the lightning. Come on, Angie."

But when they reached the gate, Angie's mulish streak surfaced. "The people who live here will ask questions," she whined. "I told you, Mary, I won't go back. You'll have to think of a story to tell them. Something smart."

"I won't have to be smart," Mary said wearily. "The house is empty, Angie. There're no lights, and everything is kind of falling down. Look."

Another flash of lightning proved her correct. The house was a farmhouse, of a type common in that part of the country—two stories high, with a steep-peaked roof. Children or tramps had broken most of the windows. The few remaining panes of glass reflected the livid flashes like blind white eyes.

Angie didn't like the look of the place, and said so in no uncertain terms. The first drops of rain spattering in the dust alongside the road ended her hesitation. Hands over her head, she ran with Mary. Before they reached the crumbling porch steps, the drops had thickened into a downpour.

Mary fell for the second time on the broken steps. She squatted on the porch, rocking back and forth in silent pain. Finally she got up, with Angie's help, and limped toward the door. It hung drunkenly on one hinge. It was so light, so rotted by time and weather, that they were able to push it back far enough to enter.

Angie took her comb from her purse. She started to run it through her damp hair. Soothed by the familiar gesture and by shelter, however poor, she spoke calmly.

"It smells funny."

"I guess it's been abandoned for a long time," Mary said, squinting into the darkness.

The house shuddered with every thunderclap. Rain trickled in through holes in the ceiling. Mary started as a chunk of wet plaster thudded to the floor. Anyhow, it was better than being outdoors.

The room was long and narrow. It was empty of furniture, but the floor was covered with debris. There was a fireplace on one wall.

"I'm hungry," Angie said.

"We've got those hamburgers. But I meant to save them for breakfast."

"We'll find a restaurant tomorrow. Let's eat now. But the hamburgers will be cold."

"I can't do anything about that," Mary said irritably.

"We could build a fire."

Mary looked at Angie in surprise. She came up with an idea so rarely that people tended to forget she could.

"Hey, yeah. There's lots of wood on the floor, and you have your lighter."

They cleared an area next to the fireplace and piled the scraps onto the hearth. Angie lit the heap. At first a lot of smoke billowed back into the room, making them cough, but finally the fire blazed up. The light was almost as welcome as the warmth, although it showed nothing but desolation—peeling wallpaper, rotted floorboards, and an ankle-deep layer of debris. Most of the latter burned nicely.

"It's funny," Mary said after dumping another load of scraps onto the fire.

"What is?" Angie was on her second hamburger. She was forced to eat it cold, after all, since her attempt to spit the first one on a stick had broken it apart.

"A lot of this wood looks like pieces of furniture," Mary said. "Like everything in the house has kind of fallen apart."

"I don't see what's so funny about that."

"Well, people don't leave their furniture when they move, do they? There's a table leg here, and enough pieces to make up a dozen chairs."

"Lucky for us," Angie said comfortably. "We can keep the fire going a long time."

"It's old wood," Mary said. "Dry. It burns fast."

It did burn fast, and it gave off a lot of heat. The part of the room near the fireplace was almost too warm. But a chill ran up Mary's back when she spoke those words. Dry . . . old . . . The syllables seemed to echo for a long time.

Angie finished her second hamburger and ate a candy bar. She wanted another, but Mary wouldn't let her have it. That was their emergency supply. If the rain continued, they might have to depend on it for longer than she had expected.

Angie accepted the decree without too much grumbling. She combed her hair again. The silky strands shone in the firelight; she spread them out across her hands, ran her fingers through the shimmering web.

"Where are we going to sleep?" she asked, stretching like a cat in the warmth.

"Where else? Right here."

"Maybe there are beds upstairs."

"If the stairs are as rotten as everything else, I wouldn't trust them. Besides," she added craftily, as Angie started to object, "you wouldn't want to sleep on any old mattresses. Mice."

"Ugh," Angie said.

After finishing her hamburger, Mary stretched out her leg and rolled up her jeans. It was no wonder her knee hurt. Angie exclaimed sympathetically. "You've got a million splinters in there."

"Yeah." Mary pulled out a couple of the longer ones. She hated things sticking into her. Mother always said she was an absolute baby about shots. Pulling out the splinters made her skin crawl. But it had to be done, and the dirt ought to be washed off. She didn't want to risk infection.

"Oh, damn," she muttered.

"Want me to pull them out?" Angie asked cheerfully. "I don't mind."

"That's not why I said *damn*. All that rain outside and we don't have any way to catch the water."

"I'm thirsty," Angie said promptly.

"Me too. And I'd like to wash my knee. Think of something."

"Who, me? You're the thinker in this family. 'Mary, she's the smart one,'" Angie mimicked their mother's voice.

"What about the cartons the hamburgers were in?"

"I threw them in the fire."

Mary said "Damn" again. "Go look in the kitchen, Angie. If the people who lived here left their furniture, maybe they left dishes too."

"I'm not going in there alone," Angie said. "There are probably rats and everything."

Mary glowered at her sister with sudden dislike. Angie looked so *fat,* sprawled out on the floor. Her thighs filled her jeans like sausage stuffing. It seemed as if she could do something for somebody once in a while, instead of expecting to be waited on all the time.

There was no use arguing about it. Stiffly Mary got to her feet. She found a splintered chair leg and lit one end of it. It sputtered and smoked, but gave enough light to let her see where she was going. Angie trailed along. She said she was afraid to be alone, and in a way Mary didn't blame her.

The kitchen wasn't hard to find; there were only four rooms downstairs. It was in a state of ruin that made the living room look tidy by comparison. Part of the ceiling had fallen, half burying the massive bulk of an old cookstove. There was no refrigerator, unless a heap of rusty metal and rotting wood had once served that function. An icebox, Mary thought—the kind that had big chunks of real ice, instead of electricity, to keep things cold.

In the debris along the wall, where shelves had collapsed, spilling their contents onto the floor, she found one unbroken cup and a dish with a chip out of the edge. They were black with grime, but the rain would wash them out.

When they reached the porch, she threw the burning stick onto the soggy grass and licked her singed fingers. The storm was passing, but it was still raining heavily. Mary washed the dishes as well as she could, and let them fill with rainwater.

It felt rather cozy to stretch out in front of the fire again. Mary began working on her knee. She got the biggest splinters out, but some of the smaller ones, deeply imbedded, were hard to get hold of, even with Angie's eyebrow tweezers. Mary was concentrating, her eyes blurred with tears; Angie was half asleep. Neither of them heard the boy coming. He was simply there, as if he had materialized out of thin air.

When Mary saw him, she let out a yelp of surprise. Angie woke up. Mary expected she'd scream, too; but when she saw Angie's mouth curve in a smile, she realized that Angie wasn't afraid of anything young and male. That was part of her trouble.

Anyhow, this boy didn't look frightening. As her pounding heart slowed, Mary saw that he was as startled as she was. He was tall and thin; his ragged clothes hung in limp folds, as if he had lost a lot of weight, or as if they had originally belonged to somebody bigger. His shaggy hair was shoulder-length; his feet were bare. He had raised his arms in front of his face, as if to shield it.

"It's okay," Mary said. "I guess you came in to get out of the rain, like us, didn't you? Come over to the fire."

The boy obeyed. His bare feet, stepping lightly, made no sound on the dusty floor. His eyes were fixed on Mary. They were dark eyes—she saw that as he came closer, out of the shadows; saw that his face, exposed when he lowered his protecting arms, was long and thin, with cheekbones that stood out sharply under the sunken pits of the eye sockets. His mouth was a clown's mouth, too long for the framework of his hollow cheeks, curving down at the corners.

He stopped a little distance from Mary; his eyes narrowed as he continued to study her. Then, as if some silent message had passed from her to him, he smiled.

Mary caught her breath. That was why his face had looked wrong. The wide lips were generously cut, designed for laughter. When his mouth curved up, all his other features fell into their proper places and proportions. But he was awfully thin. . . .

"My name's Rob," he said. His voice was soft, with a queer little hesitation.

"I'm Mary. This is Angie."

But Angie, disconcerted by a boy who looked at Mary instead of at her, had turned her back.

"Hello," Rob said gravely.

"Sit down if you want to."

"Thank you." Rob sat, crossing his legs. The soles of his feet were covered by a thick, hardened layer of skin. He must have gone barefoot for months, maybe years, Mary thought.

"You hurt yourself," he said, looking at Mary's knee.

"I fell down." Mary laughed self-consciously. "I'm the clumsy one, always falling over my own feet."

Rob did not laugh. "I bet it hurts. Why don't you pull out them splinters?"

"I'm chicken," Mary admitted. "I got out as many as I could, but . . ."

He took the tweezers from her hand. It was the lightest, gentlest movement; she scarcely felt the touch of the metal tips as he plucked out the splinters.

"I think that's most of 'em," he said finally. "You better wash it off now. You got some cloth or something?"

"I guess I could tear up a shirt."

But her pack yielded nothing that would serve. The clothes were all knits, except for an extra pair of jeans. Rob exclaimed with admiration over the T-shirts.

"Say, that's pretty. 'Specially that one with the birds and flowers. You don't wanna spoil that. Maybe I can find some old thing around here."

With the same light, almost furtive movements, he slipped out of the room.

"Boy," Angie said. "Boy, you really are a hypocrite, you know that?"

Mary started. Crazy as it might sound, she had almost forgotten about Angie.

"What do you mean?"

"Always lecturing *me* about picking up men," Angie said. "You practically fell all over him."

"You're just mad because he didn't look at you," Mary said.

"Ha!" Angie registered amused contempt. "I wouldn't want him to look at me. He's weird. Ugly. He talks funny—"

"That's the way they talk around here," Mary said coldly. "You're so ignorant, you think everybody but you talks funny. He's nice. I like him."

"Mary." Angie reached out her hand. Her face had lost its healthy color. Even in the firelight she looked pale. "Mary, he really is weird. There's something funny about him."

"Funny, weird—is that all you can say? You shut up, do you hear me? I don't want you hurting his feelings."

The warning was delivered just in time. Rob was back, carrying something. He held it out to Mary. It was an old calico shirt, faded so badly that the original print was almost gone.

"It's clean," he said anxiously. "I washed it myself. It's too small for me, anyways. You go on, tear it up."

Mary would have objected, but it was obvious that the garment was far too small for Rob. It must have been bought for him when he was thirteen or fourteen, before he had shot up to his present height.

"You been carrying this around with you?" she asked as she began to tear the cloth. "I wouldn't have bothered packing anything this old."

"No, it was upstairs," Rob said calmly.

Angie made a small sound, deep in her throat. Mary stared, a strip of cloth dangling from her fingers.

"Upstairs? You mean, you—"

"I useta live here," Rob said. "I was away for a long time, but I come back. They—they was all gone when I come. Musta moved away. . . ." His forehead wrinkled; for a moment the dark eyes went blank, like those of a sleepwalker. Then he smiled. "Sure is nice to have company. It's been lonesome."

That radiant smile dispelled Mary's uneasiness. She started dabbing at her knee.

"We ran away too," she said. "But we aren't going back."

"How come you run away?" Rob asked.

"Well, see, our father died . . ." Mary began.

She paused, waiting for the sympathetic comment that should have followed. She was a little taken aback when Rob nodded and said, "Mine too."

"Really?"

"He was killed in the war."

"Vietnam? Ours died of a heart attack." Mary realized it sounded kind of flat. A heart attack wasn't nearly as romantic or tragic as death in battle. She went on, "Then mother got married again. We have a stepfather."

"Me too."

"You're kidding."

"I guess they ain't that scarce," Rob said. "Stepfathers, I mean."

He smiled tentatively, to indicate he wasn't making fun of her, just joking. Mary's suspicions dissolved. He was right, stepfathers weren't uncommon.

"He was Pa's friend, in the war," Rob explained. "He brung Pa's things home, after it was over. Then he just . . . stayed. Ma had to have a man around. Woman can't run a farm by herself. I was too small to help." He paused, scraping at a frayed spot on his faded pants. Then he asked, "Was he mean to you? Your stepfather?"

"George? He was nice at first," Mary said darkly. "To lull our suspicions. Lately he's been on our backs all the time. Discipline, discipline, that's all we heard. Last week was the last straw. He said Angie should be sent away to school. Some awful boarding school where they make you get up at seven o'clock and have room checks and study hall every night, and no dates unless the boy has a certified letter from the President of the United States. . . ."

Rob was listening sympathetically, his flexible mouth reflecting her indignation; but somehow the description of the horrors of boarding school lacked drama, even to Mary. She added, with genuine distress, "We've always been together. You'd think that would make them happy, that we like each other. Most sisters fight all the time. We never . . . Well, we don't fight much. But George said we weren't good for each other. He said Angie depended on me too much, and I wasn't making friends of my own because I was always with her. . . ." Rob was looking bewildered. Mary gave it up. "You wouldn't understand," she said. "I guess girls have different problems from boys. What was the matter with your stepfather?"

"He useta lick me a lot. But it wasn't that so much, it was—"
Angie giggled.

"Lick you?" she repeated.

"Shut up," Mary snapped.

"You shouldn't talk mean to your little sister," Rob said reproachfully.

It was Mary's turn to laugh.

"She's not my little sister, she's my big sister. But she doesn't understand a lot of things. You mean, your stepfather actually hit you? You didn't have to put up with that. There are laws."

"Laws?"

"To protect kids from being beaten," Mary said impatiently. "Even back here in the boonies you must have heard of them. If he really hurt you—"

"Oh, he useta lay it on pretty good," Rob said matter-of-factly. And then, before Mary had any inkling of what he meant to do, he swung around and flipped up his shirt.

For a moment there was no sound in the room except the drip of rain and the crackle of the flames. Then Angie let out a gasp of hysterical laughter.

They were old scars, long healed; but it was obvious that the ridged patterns were not the product of a single beating but of systematic, long-range abuse. The play of firelight and shadow on Rob's back made them look even worse than they were.

Rob let his shirt fall, and turned. At the sight of Mary's face his mouth dropped miserably.

"Say, I didn't mean to make you feel bad. It don't hurt, honest. I'd almost forgot about it till you started talking about—"

"Forgot *that?*"

"Well, it's my head," Rob said apologetically. "It got hurt. . . . I don't remember so good since then. Seems like I forget a lot of things."

"Did your stepfather hit you on the head too?"

"He didn't much care where he hit me," Rob said with a touch of wry humor. "He was usually likkered up when he done it."

"Let me see," Mary said.

"Not if it makes you feel bad."

"It won't make me feel bad." Mary could not have explained why she felt the need to see for herself. Her reasons had nothing in common with the ghoulish interest that had drawn Angie closer.

"Okay," Rob said obediently. He bowed his head and parted his untidy brown hair. The raised scar stood up like a ridge of splintered bone.

Mary knew she mustn't upset him by any further expressions of distress, but as he sat patiently awaiting her comment, his head bowed and his long, dirty fingers passive in his tumbled hair, her eyes filled with tears. She put out her hand.

Suddenly Rob was on his feet, some distance away. His eyes were narrowed, and his thin chest rose and fell with his agitated breathing.

"Don't touch me," he whispered. "You mustn't touch me."

"I didn't mean any harm," Mary said. Two tears spilled over and left muddy tracks through the grime on her cheeks. "I only wanted—"

"I know." The boy's taut body relaxed. "I thank you. But you mustn't . . ."

Slowly, step by step, he began to back away.

Mary rose to her knees, ignoring the pain.

"Don't go away!"

"I'll come right back." He smiled at her but continued to retreat. He faded into the shadows in the open doorway.

As soon as he was gone, Angie flung herself at her sister, her fingers clawing at Mary's arm.

"Let's get out of here, Mary. Hurry. Quick, before he comes back—"

"Are you crazy?" Mary tried to free her arm, but Angie hung on.

"I'm not crazy, he is! Can't you see he's some kind of psycho? The way he talks . . . All that about forgetting things, and those awful scars . . . He's a homicidal maniac, like on TV. He'll kill us—"

"No," Mary said. "No, he wouldn't hurt anybody."

"How do you know?"

"I know. Look, Angie, you stop that kind of talk. You haven't got any sense about people. Some of the guys you used to go out with—"

"Oh, so that's it," Angie said. "You think you've got yourself a boyfriend. First time anybody looks at you . . . That shows he's crazy." She tossed her head so that the long, shining locks flared out. "Just don't try anything. Even if you think I'm asleep, you can't get away with any funny business."

Mary stared at her sister. As the meaning of Angie's speech penetrated, she felt a deep flush warm her face.

"You're disgusting, Angie, you know that?"

Angie began to cry. "That's an awful thing to say," she sobbed. "I'm scared, and hungry, and cold, and all you can say—" The rest of the words were lost in gulping sobs.

"All right, all right," Mary said. "Stop bawling. We can't leave here; it's still raining, and it's pitch-dark, and I don't know where we are. I'll sit up all night and protect you from that fierce, dangerous boy. Go to sleep and stop worrying."

It took the last of the hamburgers to stop Angie's moans. When she had eaten it, she curled up by the fire, and after an interval her sobs smoothed out into soft snores. Mary didn't feel sleepy. She looked at her sister's huddled form and felt as if she were looking at a stranger.

It wasn't the first time Angie had made cracks about her not having boyfriends or dates, but never before had she expressed her malice so openly. And to suggest that Rob would . . . Mary felt her face get hot again, this time with anger. Nobody but a stupid fool could think of Rob that way. He was too pathetic. All he wanted was kindness and companionship, and some response to the gentleness that had miraculously survived the terrible treatment he had received.

He had been gone a long time. Maybe he had gone for good. The idea left Mary feeling a little sick. Had their unthinking cruelty driven him out into the rain and darkness, away from even the poor refuge he had found? But when she looked at the doorway, he was there, watching her.

"I thought you weren't coming back," she said.

"I said I would." Rob came forward, stepping softly. He jerked his head toward Angie. "She asleep?"

"Yes."

"I tried to find some blankets, or something to keep you

warm. I guess everything around here is just too old or too dirty. I'm sorry."

"It's warm enough, with the fire." Mary tossed another handful of wood on it. The flames leapt. "But thanks for trying. Where do you sleep?"

"Upstairs. But I don't sleep much." Rob sat down a little distance from her. "If you want to go to sleep, I'll sort of keep an eye on things."

"What's there to watch out for?"

"Well, there's rats," Rob said calmly. "They wouldn't hurt you, but I know girls is scared of rats."

"Ugh." Mary shivered. "I hate them."

"They ain't so bad. They only bite people when they're scared or hungry. Right smart animals, rats are. I had one for a pet oncet."

"Really? I knew a boy who had a pet rat. It was a white one."

"Mine was brown. I called him Horatius, after that fella in the poem."

Mary didn't know what poem he was talking about, and she didn't want to admit her ignorance, so she changed the subject.

"What are you going to do, Rob? You can't stay here."

"I have to."

"No, you don't. You could—you could come with us."

"With you?"

"Yes." Mary felt herself blushing again. She lowered her eyes, cursing Angie; if Angie hadn't put ideas into her head, she wouldn't be embarrassed. Tracing patterns in the dust of the floor with her forefinger, she went on rapidly, "We're going to get jobs. You could work too. We could have an apartment—maybe even a little house. . . ."

"I sure would like to," Rob said. "I'd like to be with you. I never knew a girl like you before. I didn't know you, did I? Seems as if I did somehow. I forget so much. . . ."

Mary looked up sharply. Her cheeks were still flaming; as her eyes met Rob's she forgot to be self-conscious. He was speaking the simple, literal truth, as he felt it.

"No," she said, just as simply. "I never met you. But it's funny, I feel that way too. As if we had known each other someplace . . . sometime. . . ."

For a long, suspended moment, they looked at each other, not speaking, because there was no need to speak. Then Rob's mobile, expressive face lengthened. He bowed his head.

"No," he muttered. "I can't do it. I been telling you lies. Not lies, exactly, but not the truth, neither. I—I didn't run away from here. I was took from here. It was some other place I run away from, some place a long, long ways from here."

Mary felt as if a giant hand had clamped over her ribs, squeezing the breath out of her lungs. She stared at Rob's droop-ing head. His long, curved lashes cast delicate shadows across his bony cheeks.

So Angie had been right—for once.

Rob's stumbling, reluctant confession was like the missing

piece in a jigsaw puzzle. The pattern was clear now. But then, it had been pretty obvious all along. Angie had seen it, and she herself would have recognized it if she had not refused to do so.

Rob was . . . different. Not crazy, not any of those ugly words Angie had used. He was sick; and no wonder, after what had been done to him. The place he had run away from was probably an institution, a kind of hospital. Some of those places were pretty bad; she had seen stories about them on TV. He must have been in—that place—for years, long enough for the house to fall into ruin after his family had moved away, abandoning him. But he had returned, like a sick animal, to the only place he knew, and his hurt mind couldn't understand what had happened.

Rob's head sank lower, till she could see only a mop of tumbled brown hair. In a sudden, final flash of insight Mary knew that Angie had been wrong, after all—Angie and those others who had locked Rob up. Rob's mind had been damaged, like his bruised body, but its essential quality had not been changed. He was still gentle, considerate of others, oddly innocent. He wouldn't hurt anybody; he was too vulnerable himself.

She wanted to touch him, to reassure him. But she remembered his reaction the first time she had reached out.

"It's okay," she said softly. "I understand. It's all right."

Rob looked up.

"No," he said. He spoke with difficulty. There were long

pauses between phrases as he went on. "I guess it ain't all right. It's all wrong. I don't suppose I can explain it. I don't understand so good myself. But I understand better than I did. Having somebody to talk to—somebody like you, who listens, and don't yell or get mad. . . . All I know is, I can't come with you. I gotta go back there. It's no good running away from things."

He saw her face change and was quick to reassure her. "Say, now, I didn't mean you. You were right to run away when they treated you so bad. Guess you wouldn't do anything wrong, you're too smart. But I'm kind of mixed up. Seems like I'm always doing the wrong thing; seems like running away was another wrong thing. It wasn't a bad place, you know. They wanted to help me. If I go back and let them do what it was they wanted . . . Maybe later you and I could . . . You aren't mad, are you? Mary?"

It was the first time he had said her name. Mary couldn't speak, but she shook her head and managed to shape a watery smile. Rob smiled back at her.

"You look awful tired," he said, with a new note of gentle authority in his voice. "You lay down and get some sleep. I'll keep watch."

Suddenly she was tired—tired and strangely cold, as if she had worked hard through a long day and night of winter. She gathered up all the loose scraps that lay within reach, and heaped them on the fire. As it blazed up, she stretched out with her back to its warmth. She wanted to watch Rob; she was afraid he might try to sneak away while she slept. She was too tired to argue, but she hadn't given up. In the morning, when she wasn't so sleepy, she would try again to convince him.

Maybe he needed help, but the place he had run away from couldn't be the right place. George would find a place. George was a lawyer; he knew about things like that. George would help.

She was too drowsy to realize that she had reached a decision until after it was irrevocably fixed in her mind. Yes, she would go home—crawl back in disgrace. It wouldn't be pleasant. She'd be grounded for weeks; probably she would have to have boring sessions with a dumb psychologist or counselor. Mother would cry, and Angie. . . Angie would have to take care of herself. Anything, so long as Rob got the help he needed. Anything, so she didn't lose him.

He was still there. Her eyes closed and her breathing slowed. The last thing she saw before exhaustion claimed her was the play of firelight on Rob's thin, thoughtful face.

She awoke to a nightmare—a swirling, smoky blackness shot with tongues of flame; air she couldn't breathe; and a hoarse, wordless shouting. The voice was unrecognizable; it might even have been her own. She knew she must be dreaming, because she couldn't move. It was a relief when the blackness overcame the fiery light and swallowed her.

She came fully awake much later, with hard hands shaking her and a face close to hers.

"Rob," she croaked, but it wasn't Rob; the face was that of a man she had never seen before—brown and weather-wrinkled, with parallel scarlike lines framing his thin-lipped mouth.

"This one's all right," he said. His voice sounded angry. "What about the other one?"

If there was an answer, Mary didn't hear it. Feeling dizzy and slightly sick to her stomach, she closed her eyes. When she opened them again, the man was gone. She raised herself on one elbow and looked around.

She was lying in the long, wet grass in front of the house. Her clothes were soaked, and she was shivering in a sharp breeze—a dawn breeze. The sky was streaked with light beyond the chimneys of the house. The house was burning.

There was a horrifying beauty about the way it burned. Long veils of fire rose like creatures trying to break free of earth. Rosy flame spouted from the empty windows and wreathed crimson blossoms around the chimneys. Then the roof fell in with a giant gush of flame and sparks, and her dazed senses came fully to life.

"Angie." She gasped and staggered to her feet.

Before she had time to panic, she saw her sister, flat on the grass a few feet away. A man was bending over her. As Mary stumbled toward them, the man looked up. He was not the man she had seen before; he was older. A stubble of white beard frosted his jaws, and when he spoke, she saw that his teeth were brown, with gaps in their rows.

"Friend o' yours?"

"My sister."

"She'll do," the old man said cheerfully. "Swallowed some smoke, but I reckon she'll be all right."

Then Mary remembered.

"Rob. Rob! Where—"

She spun around. The old man straightened, one hand clutching the small of his back.

"Was there somebody else with you, girl?"

"Yes. Rob. Didn't you find him? Oh, please . . ."

The old man's silence was answer enough.

Mary ran toward the incandescent bed of coals that had once been a house. The daylight had strengthened; against the dawn, the blackened chimney stood up like a gaunt sentinel. She heard the old man shout but did not stop running till someone grabbed her. She had forgotten the other man. When she tried to struggle, he slapped her hard. The older man came up, panting.

"Don't hit her, Frank."

"Too bad her folks didn't tan her hide a long time ago," Frank said angrily. "Damned spoiled brats. Wouldn't a been no fire if they hadn't set it. Lucky they didn't kill themselves."

"Frank, she says there was another youngster with them. A boy."

The hands that held Mary did not relax their grip, but when Frank spoke again, his voice had lost its hard edge.

"Didn't find anybody else. If he was in there . . ."

The three stared silently at the fiery grave of the house. Then the old man said gently, "Maybe he got out, child. Maybe he drug you out. Frank saw the smoke when he went to feed the stock, but we didn't get here till the place was blazing. Found you gals outside on the grass. Reckon your friend ran and hid when he saw us. Sure, that's what must of happened."

The words should have consoled Mary, because they made sense. She knew she hadn't dragged Angie out of the house; she couldn't even remember walking out herself. Strangely, she felt no emotion, neither horror nor loss of hope. She looked at the old man through the lank locks of hair that hung over her face, and his eyes shifted away.

"Better take 'em home, Frank. You wanna go fetch the car?"

"Why can't they walk?" Frank demanded.

"Other one's still snoring," the old man said with a faint grin. "You kin carry her if you want; she's too fat for me to hoist."

"All right," Frank said grudgingly. "Damned spoiled runaway brats, burning down a house. . . ."

"Maybe it's just as well," the old man said. The eyes of the two men met in a long, meaningful glance. Then Frank shrugged and set off across the lawn. When Mary looked in that direction, she saw chimneys beyond the trees. They had been close to shelter and human help. . . . Not that they would have sought it out.

The old man bent stiffly over Angie's recumbent form.

"She's all right," he said. "Sleeping it off."

"I'm sorry," Mary said. "About the house. It was raining so hard, I never thought it could catch fire."

"Don't suppose you thought at all," the old man said sarcastically. "Inside of the place was bone-dry and rotten."

"Why did you say that—about it being just as well the house was burned?"

The old man shrugged and looked away.

"Been falling for years. No good to anybody."

"Why wasn't it any good to anybody? Why did the people who owned it let it fall apart? Who lived there? What—what happened to them?"

"Full of questions, ain't you?" The old man grinned, but the glance he gave her from under his shaggy white brows was oblique and sly. Suddenly, though she could not have explained why, she had to know the answers to the questions she had asked.

"Why?" she demanded, her voice loud and shrill. "What was wrong with the house?"

The old man licked his lips. He glanced over his shoulder at the blackened ruins.

"Folks said it was haunted," he mumbled. "I seen lights there myself. Mighta been tramps, but . . ."

"Haunted," Mary repeated. She shivered. The early-morning air was cold, and she was wet to the bone.

As if the word had been a plug in his mind that held back speech, the old man became garrulous. After all, it was a good story and she was a fresh audience.

"There was a murder there one time. Years ago, it was. The widow moved away afterward, took the other kids with her. Place changed hands a couple of times; but nobody could live in that house for long. State took it over for taxes finally. Couldn't even rent it, people knew the story—"

He broke off, eyeing her uneasily. Mary had stopped listening. Now she repeated the phrase that had twisted into her mind like a knife.

"Other kids," she said in a strangled voice. "She took the other. . . Who was it who was killed?"

"The father," the old man said reluctantly. "Stepfather, he was, really. Say, you look kind of peaked. Maybe I better not—"

"Who killed him?"

"Here's Frank with the car," the old man said, looking relieved. "Come on."

The car had stopped by the tumbledown fence. Frank got out, holding a blanket.

"Mother says bring 'em right to the house," he said, looking at Angie. "Think you can take her feet, Granddad, if I—"

"Who was it?" Mary begged. "Who killed him?"

Frank gave the old man a disapproving look.

"You been telling her that story? Shame on you, Granddad. That's what's wrong with kids today, they hear too many stories about killing and stuff." He turned on Mary. "Just you forget all that. You oughta be thinking about this gal here—and your folks, bet they're worried sick about you. Get in the car."

Angie was coming out of her stupor, but she was always a good sleeper. Once in the car, she snuggled into the blanket, muttered something, and closed her eyes.

The two men stood staring at the remains of the house.

"So it's gone," the old man said. "Yep. Just as well. They say fire's a cleaning thing. If ever a place needed cleaning, that one did. And if ever a man deserved killing . . ."

"You never even knew him," Frank said.

"I heard Pop talk about him. Drunken brute he was, used to beat that poor woman to a pulp, and the kids . . . Nowadays they'd say the boy wasn't in his right mind. Not responsible."

"That's the trouble with nowadays. Nobody's ever responsible."

"Maybe so. But when you keep beating on a kid, stands to reason his brain isn't gonna be right. And seeing his ma knocked around. . . Pop said it was a cruel thing, the way she turned on the boy. Wouldn't see him or say anything in his defense; even at the trial. And the way he died . . . Suicide, it was supposed to be, but the guard at the county jail was one of the Weavers, and the Weavers has always had a mean streaky. . . ."

Frank shook himself like a dog coming out of the water.

"What're we standing around talking for?" he demanded grumpily. "It's over and done with, years ago, and I'm late with the chores, thanks to these fool girls. Get in the car, Granddad."

The old man obeyed, giving Mary a strange sidelong look. She had a feeling that he had remembered the name of the boy who had died in prison so many years before. He wouldn't say anything, though. He knew, as she did, how the reasonable, everyday world would react to such a story.

A story decades old, older than Granddad himself. How

many years had it been since a certain man returned from a war—not Vietnam, she should have realized the dates were wrong. Maybe the horrors of that war had turned him into a drunkard and a sadist. She would never know. All she knew was that Rob had been a victim, not a killer. Just once, after years of abuse and misery, he had struck back. He hadn't meant to kill, only to defend himself and the others. She knew that as certainly as if she had been present when it happened.

As the car started forward, Mary pressed her face against the window for a last look. The sun was up and the damp grass glowed like a field of emeralds. From the dying embers trails of pale smoke rose and broke in the breeze.

When the ashes were cold, weeds and wildflowers would rise to cover the ruins. Animals would burrow and raise their young. But Rob would not come again. He had gone back, as she was going, but to a much more distant place. In her mind a voice said softly, "Maybe later. You and I . . ."

ABOUT THE AUTHOR

Elizabeth Peters (1927–2013) was one of the pseudonyms of American writer Barbara Louise Mertz, whose *New York Times*-bestselling Amelia Peabody mysteries are often set against historical backdrops. In 1952, Peters earned a PhD in Egyptology at the University of Chicago. She was named grand master at the inaugural Anthony Awards in 1986 and by the Mystery Writers of America in 1998. In 2003, she received the Lifetime Achievement Award at the Malice Domestic Convention.

ELIZABETH PETERS

FROM MYSTERIOUSPRESS.COM
AND OPEN ROAD MEDIA

MYSTERIOUSPRESS.COM

MYSTERIOUSPRESS.COM

Otto Penzler, owner of the Mysterious Bookshop in Manhattan, founded the Mysterious Press in 1975. Penzler quickly became known for his outstanding selection of mystery, crime, and suspense books, both from his imprint and in his store. The imprint was devoted to printing the best books in these genres, using fine paper and top dust-jacket artists, as well as offering many limited, signed editions.

Now the Mysterious Press has gone digital, publishing ebooks through **MysteriousPress.com**.

MysteriousPress.com offers readers essential noir and suspense fiction, hard-boiled crime novels, and the latest thrillers from both debut authors and mystery masters. Discover classics and new voices, all from one legendary source.

FIND OUT MORE AT

WWW.MYSTERIOUSPRESS.COM

FOLLOW US:

@emysteries and Facebook.com/MysteriousPressCom

MysteriousPress.com is one of a select group of publishing partners of Open Road Integrated Media, Inc.

THE MYSTERIOUS BOOKSHOP, founded in 1979, is located in Manhattan's Tribeca neighborhood. It is the oldest and largest mystery-specialty bookstore in America.

The shop stocks the finest selection of new mystery hardcovers, paperbacks, and periodicals. It also features a superb collection of signed modern first editions, rare and collectable works, and Sherlock Holmes titles. The bookshop issues a free monthly newsletter highlighting its book clubs, new releases, events, and recently acquired books.

58 Warren Street
info@mysteriousbookshop.com
(212) 587-1011
Monday through Saturday
11:00 a.m. to 7:00 p.m.

FIND OUT MORE AT:

www.mysteriousbookshop.com

FOLLOW US:

@TheMysterious and Facebook.com/MysteriousBookshop

OPEN ROAD

INTEGRATED MEDIA

Find a full list of our authors and
titles at www.openroadmedia.com

FOLLOW US
@OpenRoadMedia

Harris County Public Library
Houston, Texas

CPSIA information can be obtained
at www.ICGtesting.com
Printed in the USA
LVHW030009161118
597349LV00001B/11/P

9 781504 055512